Sea Otter Pup

written by VICTORIA MILES
illustrated by ELIZABETH GATT

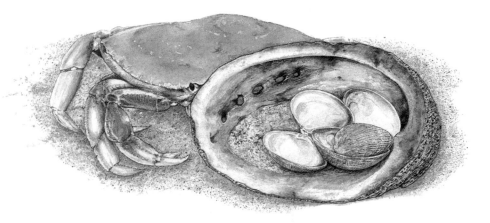

ORCA BOOK PUBLISHERS

There is a forest of seaweed in the ocean. It is a forest of kelp. At the bottom of the kelp forest, Mother sea otter searches for food.

High above, her pup is waiting. He is wrapped in a piece of kelp so he can't drift away while Mother is down below.

He bobs, floating on his back in the cold waves, holding his front paws and hind flippers above the water to keep them dry.

Pup is hungry. He is anxious for Mother to return and begins to make crying sounds to call for her.

Waaah . . . Waaah . . . Waaah . . . . Pup's voice sounds like the cry of the seagulls that soar high above him in the sky.

Suddenly Mother pops her head up above the waves. She swims to Pup and tucks him under her arm. Then she rolls over onto her back and Pup lies on her chest.

Mother has two purple sea urchins for them to share. Pup is so hungry, he snatches one of the urchins from her paws. He opens his jaws as wide as he can and bites . . .

Yipe! cries Pup. The sea urchin's spines are sharp. They hurt his mouth.

Pup watches his mother. She is more careful. Purple urchins are her favourite food and she knows just how to eat them.

Using her teeth, she cracks open the hard shell and slurps out the tasty urchin. She shares a piece with Pup and he gobbles it down.

Eating sea urchins is messy. Mother and
Pup must wash. Mother sets Pup aside
and somersaults once . . .

twice . . .

three times under the ocean waves.

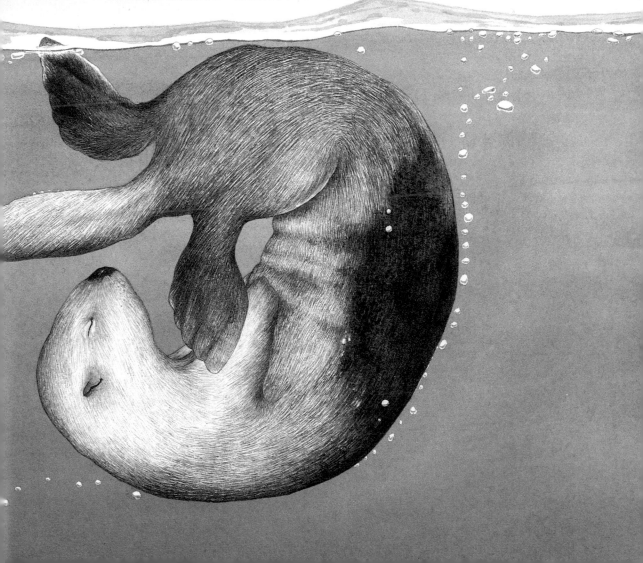

Then she washes herself. Pup tries to copy her. He rubs his head with his paws and pulls at his fur. When Mother is finished with her own grooming, she squeezes the water out of Pup's fur. She combs him with her claws and fluffs him all over.

Pup yawns. The afternoon sun is warm and he snuggles closer against Mother's chest. In a moment he is fast asleep.

Pup does not sleep for long. He is hungry again and Mother must leave him to dive for food.

They wash after every meal. Mother otter helps Pup and sometimes grooms him while he is asleep.

She will dive many more times, throughout the days and nights, to find the urchins, crabs and molluscs she needs to feed them both.

Soon Pup will begin to follow her deep down below the waves, and he will learn to find food for himself.

Sea otters (*Enhydra lutris*) were once a relatively common marine mammal throughout the coastal waters of the North Pacific. By the early 1900s, however, they had disappeared from much of their former range due to overhunting. Today the remaining sea otters of North America are protected from hunting, although they remain vulnerable to human disturbance of their habitats, gill-net fishing and most significantly, the threat of oil-spills.

The author and illustrator gratefully acknowledge Marianne Riedman, Ph.D., and Marisa Nichini for their expertise and assistance in preparing this book.

Publication assistance provided by The Canada Council.

Orca Book Publishers
PO Box 5626, Station B
Victoria, BC Canada
V8R 6S4

Orca Book Publishers
PO Box 468
Custer, WA   USA
98240-0468

10 9 8 7 6 5

Canadian Cataloguing in Publication Data
Miles, Victoria, 1966 —
     Sea otter pup

     ISBN 1-55143-002-9
     1. Sea otter — Juvenile literature.   I.
Gatt, Elizabeth, 1951—   II. Title.
QL737.C25M54 1993   j599.74'447   C93-091564-X

Design by Christine Toller
Printed and bound in Hong Kong